It's Halloween, Little Monster

by Helen Ketteman

two lions

illustrated by Bonnie Leick

Published by Two Lions, New York

www.apub.com

Amazon, the Amazon logo, and Two Lions are trademarks of Amazon.com, Inc., or its affiliates.

ISBN-13: 9781542092081 (hardcover)
ISBN-10: 1542092086 (hardcover)

The illustrations are rendered in watercolor.

Book design by AndWorld Design
Printed in China

First Edition

10 9 8 7 6 5 4 3 2 1

To all adorable Little Monsters everywhere
—H. K.

To Zoe and Zepplin, the original Batdogs
—B. L.

IT'S HERE, LITTLE MONSTER!
Almost time to go out.
Hurry! Get dressed!
There are creatures about.

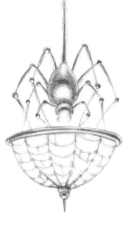

Look at you, Little Monster—
dressed all in green.
You're a Martian from space
on your **FIRST HALLOWEEN**.

All set to go!
You see things that are SCARY?
A pirate, a witch,
a creature that's hairy?

Don't fret, Little Monster.
See there in the street?
That's not really a ghost—
it's a kid in a sheet!

Shine your light, Little Monster.
Let's head down the street.
We'll knock on some doors
and say "**TRICK OR TREAT!**"

What, Little Monster?
You heard something howl?
It's Halloween night,
when **SPOOKY** things prowl.

But you shouldn't be nervous.
Your papa is here.
And together we're brave.
There's nothing to fear.

What's that, Little Monster?
Something scary swooshed by?
Oh no! It's a vampire—
a big, creepy guy!

Hold your bag tight
and don't make a fuss.
Now let's run past him FAST!

WHEW! He didn't get US!

You hear a weird noise?
You're right—it sounds strange.

Oh **NO!** Look at **THAT!**
Zombies in chains!

QUICK! Walk like a zombie without a brain stem.

They won't bother us
if we act just like them.

First, zombies. Now ghosts.
No shivers and shakes?

Oh, I see why you're brave—

There's one final house
across from the park.
The scariest one yet,
ALL SPOOKY AND DARK.

What's on the porch?
OH! A goblin is perched!
He might try to grab us
with a quick surprise lurch.

The yard's full of graves.
This could be tough.
Shall we trick-or-treat here?
Will you be **BRAVE** enough?

Come along, Little Monster.
BE STRONG—JUST LIKE ME.

It won't be so scary.
Follow Papa—you'll see.

YIKES,
Little Monster!
That gave me a fright!
Your papa got scared
this Halloween night!

31901066194202